Once upon a time there lived a lonely clockmaker called Gepetto. "Oh, I wish I had children," he sighed. It was then that he decided to make a wooden puppet which he called Pinocchio. It worked beautifully!

That night, when the clockmaker was asleep, Pinocchio was dancing on a chair when a strange light appeared and a voice said, "I am the Blue Fairy and I can make you a real boy. You must however, be a good son." "Father," shouted Pinocchio, wakening the clockmaker, "I can speak like any other boy."

The next morning, Pinocchio promised his father he would go to school. Along the way, he met a fox and a cat, two naughty villains. They were going to the circus, and they persuaded Pinocchio to go with them.

On the way, they chatted non-stop about clowns and wild animals. The fox and the cat decided to sell Pinocchio to the circus owner for a good price. Poor Pinocchio! On seeing the circus he shouted, "Hurray - Down with school."

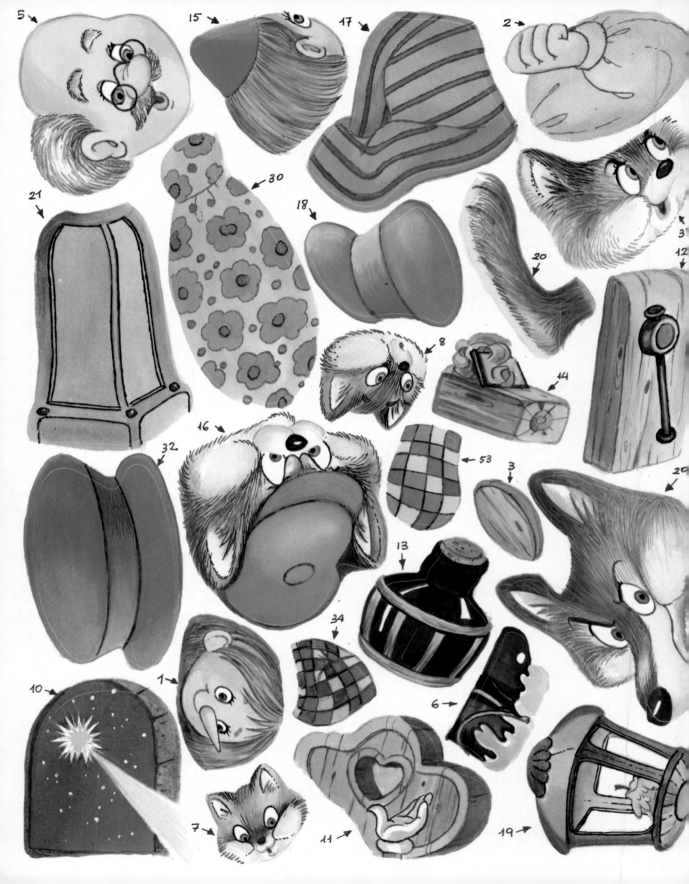

Pinocchio watched the whole show in amazement, while the sly fox and the cat talked to the circus owner. They told him how cleverly Pinocchio could sing and dance, and after the owner had paid them, they left the poor puppet there alone.

Pinocchio soon realized what had happened when the fat man pushed him into a cage. "Take pity on me!" cried Pinocchio. "You cannot escape from here. I will be rich, ha, ha!" chuckled the circus owner. Alas, Pinocchio cried as never before.

Suddenly, Pinocchio's nose began to grow, and it was then that he remembered his good father Gepetto. "Forgive me," wailed the puppet, and at that moment the light appeared again, making his nose shrink and the iron cage vanish.

The Blue Fairy
pitied him but
said, "Pinocchio,
do not forget this
lesson." Pinocchio
promised to be good
and climbed out of the
window. He ran towards
Gepetto's house, crying to
be forgiven. The kind
clockmaker did so at once,
and Pinocchio immediately
turned into a real boy.
Pinocchio and Gepetto lived
happily ever after.